D0031195

Andy
and
Tamika

Andy Russell's other (mis)adventures:

Andy
and
Tamika

David A. Adler

With illustrations by
Will Hillenbrand

Gulliver Books
Harcourt, Inc.
Orlando Austin New York
San Diego Toronto London

www.HarcourtBooks.com

First Gulliver Books paperback edition 1999

Gulliver Books is a trademark of Harcourt, Inc.,
registered in the United States of America and/or other jurisdictions.

The Library of Congress has cataloged an earlier edition as follows:
Adler, David A.
Andy and Tamika/by David A. Adler; illustrated by Will Hillenbrand.
p. cm.
"Gulliver Books."
Summary: Preoccupied with the impending arrival of his new baby brother or
sister, fourth grader Andy gets in lots of trouble at home and at school.
[1. Babies—Fiction. 2. Brothers and sisters—Fiction. 3. Family life—Fiction.
4. Schools—Fiction.] I. Hillenbrand, Will, ill. II. Title.
III. Series: Adler, David A. Andy Russell series.
PZ7.A2615An 1999
[Fic]—dc21 98-39423
ISBN 0-15-201735-6
ISBN 0-15-205446-4 pb

Text set in Century Old Style
Designed by Kaelin Chappell

C E G H F D B

Printed in the United States of America

For Eitan,
a great reader,
a great thinker,
and a great son

Contents

Chapter 1
Cobalt Nickel Russell

Grover, Andy Russell thought. *Grover Russell.*
He wrote that in his notebook.

Or we could call him Trevor, or Justin, or Michael, or Sherlock.

Andy wrote those names in his notebook, too.
Then he crossed out Sherlock. He didn't like the
sound of Sherlock Russell.

Andy looked at the names he was considering
for his brother. Of course, the baby wasn't born

yet, and it might be a girl. . . . Suddenly he had what he thought was a great idea.

We'll call him Russell! That could be his first name *and* his last name. *He'll be Russell Russell! He won't have to worry if he is filling out a form and it says "Write your last name first" or "Write your first name first." It will always be the same. Russell Russell.*

"Andrew!"

His teacher, Ms. Roman, was calling to him.

"Are you aware," Ms. Roman asked, "that we're having a test on fractions this Thursday?"

"We are?" Andy asked.

He didn't remember hearing about a test. He also didn't remember learning very much about fractions.

"Yes, we are," Ms. Roman told him. "And there will be questions like this on the test." She took a sheet of paper off her desk and read from it. "How would four people share five apples?"

Ms. Roman looked up from the paper and directly at Andy. She waited.

"Well, Andrew! Do you have an answer?"

"Me?" Andy asked.

It seemed to Andy that everyone in the class was looking at him.

What do they expect me to say? Andy wondered. *I don't know any of this stuff.*

"Well?" Ms. Roman asked.

Andy looked down at his desk and said softly, "I don't like apples."

A few children in the class laughed.

"Very cute," Ms. Roman said. "Now please answer the question."

"Well," Andy said slowly. "I would give each person one apple, and when they all finished eating, I would ask, 'Who wants another one?'"

"I know!" Stacy Ann Jackson called out as she raised her hand. She sat right in front of Andy.

"Yes, Stacy Ann?" Ms. Roman asked.

"I would give each person one and a quarter apples."

"Very good," Ms. Roman said.

RRRR!

The bell rang. It was time for lunch.

Stacy Ann Jackson turned and told Andy, "You really should pay attention in class. If you did, you might get some good grades." Then she smiled and added, "But not as good as mine."

Stacy Ann Jackson put her pencil in her pencil case, closed her notebook, unzipped her backpack, and took out her lunch bag.

She looked at Andy and smiled.

Andy waited.

Stacy Ann folded her arms and kept looking at Andy.

What is she waiting for? Andy wondered.

She smiled again.

She wants to walk to lunch with me, Andy decided. *That's why she's waiting. Then she'll probably want to sit with me. Yuck!*

Andy opened his notebook. He pretended to be reading something.

"It's upside down," Stacy Ann told Andy. "And I'm too hungry to wait for you," she said, and walked out.

Andy looked at his notebook. It *was* upside down! He dropped it on his desk, grabbed his lunch bag, and left the room.

Andy walked slowly through the halls.

He entered the cafeteria, and Bruce Jeffries called to him, "Over here! Over here! I saved you a seat."

Andy walked to the table nearest the windows

4

and sat across from his best friends, Tamika Anderson and Bruce.

"You know what I would have said? You know what?" Bruce asked.

Andy took the sandwich out of his lunch bag, unwrapped the aluminum foil, and asked Bruce, "What would you have said?"

"When Ms. Roman asked how to share the apples, I would have said, 'I'd make applesauce.'"

"That would have been funny," Andy told him. Then he shook his head and added, "You might have thought that, but you wouldn't have said it. I'm the only one who says whatever he's thinking. That's why I get in so much trouble."

Andy bit into his sandwich.

"Agh!" he shouted, then dropped his sandwich, grabbed on to his neck with both hands, and pretended to choke himself. "This cream cheese is so dry. I need something to drink."

Andy got up and went to the cafeteria counter and bought a container of milk. On his way back to the table, he passed the window.

"Hey, look!" he called to Tamika and Bruce. "There's a kitten hiding near the outside trash cans. I bet she's hungry."

Andy stepped closer to the window and said, "Don't worry. I'll feed you."

Andy returned to his table.

He took two quick bites of his sandwich. He put the cookies his mother gave him for dessert in his shirt pocket, gave his apple to Bruce, and said, "Let's go out."

"What about your milk?" Bruce asked.

"I'm giving it to the kitten. On the way back to class, I'll drink from the water fountain."

Tamika and Bruce quickly finished eating their lunches. On their way outside, they all threw their empty lunch bags in the large garbage can by the door. Andy took the top piece of bread off what was left of his sandwich and threw that away, too.

"Just wait there," Andy said as he walked past the trash. "I've got a treat for you."

"People are looking," Bruce whispered to Andy. "They think you're talking to the garbage."

"I don't care," Andy said.

He led his friends to a quiet corner of the playground, past all the children who were running, jumping rope, and playing ball. He tore the top off the milk container and put it on the ground. He carefully placed the bread he was holding next to the milk, with the cream cheese side facing up.

"Come on," he whispered to Tamika and Bruce. "Let's move away."

They walked to the fence and waited.

The kitten ran to the milk. She lapped it up and then pushed over the container with her paws so she could get the few remaining drops. Then she licked the cream cheese off the bread.

Andy admired the kitten's dark gray fur and white face, chest, and feet.

"Isn't she beautiful?" he asked.

While Andy, Tamika, and Bruce watched the kitten, Tamika told Andy, "The Perlmans asked if we could take care of their house and water their plants while they're away."

"Yeah, sure," Andy said. He was still watching the kitten.

"They're leaving the lights and radio on timers, so people will think there's someone home."

"Did you see that?" Andy asked. "She drank all the milk and ate all the cream cheese. She must have been real hungry."

Tamika looked at Andy. "I told the Perlmans,"

she went on, "we'd feed their koalas and kanga-roos and vacuum out their pockets, too."

"Sure," Andy said.

"Wow!" Bruce exclaimed. "I didn't know the Perlmans had pets. And you get to clean out the kangaroos' pockets! You're so lucky. The Perl-mans must be great foster parents."

"They're real nice," Tamika told him. "But the only pet they have is a goldfish named Sylvia. I just said that about the koalas and kangaroos to see if Andy was listening."

"Oh."

"Yeah," Andy said. "I'm sorry I wasn't listening. I was watching the kitten."

Tamika's parents had been in a car accident. While they were recovering in a rehabilitation center, Tamika lived next door to Andy, at the Perlmans'. But the Perlmans would soon be going to South America for a year, for their work. While they were away, Tamika would live with Andy and his family.

"I'm going to miss them," Tamika said. "I'm re-ally going to miss them."

RRRR!

The school bell rang. Lunchtime was over.

"Don't walk near the kitten," Andy told Tamika and Bruce. "We don't want to scare her away."

In the hall, just outside of the cafeteria, Andy took a drink from the water fountain.

"There should be a fountain outside," Andy said, "with milk, for stray cats and kittens."

Bruce shook his head and said, "I don't think so. Cats and kittens wouldn't be able to turn the knob with their paws."

"You may be right," Andy teased.

In the afternoon science lesson, Ms. Roman told the class, "Magnets attract only certain metals— iron, steel, nickel, and cobalt."

Cobalt Russell, Andy thought. *That would be an interesting name.* He wrote it in his notebook. *Or Nickel Russell.* Andy wrote that, too, and then looked at both names. *I've got it! We'll call him Cobalt Nickel Russell. Now that's a solid name, a metal name!*

"In each of these shoe boxes," Ms. Roman told the class, "are a magnet and some metal objects. When you get the box, test each object with the magnet and then record your observations in your notebook."

Ms. Roman gave a shoe box to each of the children who sat in the front of the room.

Andy watched Nicole Adams touch a soda can and a paper clip with the magnet. Then she touched her belt buckle and the braces on her teeth with it. Bruce touched his knee, chin, and nose with the magnet.

"That's unsanitary," Ms. Roman told Nicole. "And testing your nose with a magnet is just silly," she told Bruce. "If you're finished, please pass the box to the next person."

Nicole and Bruce passed the boxes to the children sitting behind them.

Andy waited for his turn to test the metals.

When Stacy Ann Jackson turned and gave Andy the shoe box, she smiled and asked him, "Were you paying attention? Do you know what to do with this?"

Andy looked in the box and asked, "Hey, where are the shoes?"

"We're doing science now," Stacy Ann Jackson told him. "You're supposed to use the magnet to test the metals."

"I know, I know," Andy said. "I was just joking."

Andy listed the metal objects in his notebook—

penny, soda can, tuna fish can, and paper clip—
and tested them. He recorded his observations
and then passed the box to the girl sitting behind
him.

After the science lesson, there was time for silent reading. Andy took a book from his backpack,
a mystery, and opened it. But he didn't read. He
thought about the baby his mother was going to
have, the kitten, and how great it would be to have
Tamika staying in his house.

After about twenty minutes, Ms. Roman told
her students to close their books. "Let's talk about
the fourth-grade carnival," she said.

"You know, it's next week, and all the money
we raise will be for the local soup kitchen—so
please bring whatever toys and books you've out-
grown for prizes. And Andy, you said you had
some gerbils we could give away."

"Some?!" Andy said. "I've got fifty of them!"

"Well, please wait until the day of the carnival
to bring them in."

"We'll need lots of big jars, one for each of the
gerbils," Andy said.

"Please bring in jars," Ms. Roman told the class.

"And make small holes in the lids," Andy said,

"so the gerbils can breathe. And if it's a mayonnaise jar, make sure it's empty. Gerbils don't like mayonnaise."

RRRR!

The school day was over.

On the ride home, Andy, Tamika, and Bruce sat together in the back of the bus, on the last seat.

"What was all that writing you were doing in class?" Tamika asked Andy.

"Just names."

"Names of what?" Tamika asked.

Bruce looked at Andy and smiled. He knew the Russells were expecting a baby, but Tamika didn't.

Tamika looked at Bruce and then at Andy.

"What?" she asked impatiently.

Last night Mom talked to Mrs. Belmont about the baby, Andy thought, *so maybe it's not a secret anymore.*

"Just a minute," Andy told Tamika.

He walked two rows up and whispered to his older sister, Rachel, "Can I tell Tamika about the baby?"

"Sure," Rachel answered. "Now Mom is telling everyone. She's beginning to gain weight and wants people to know she's pregnant and not just getting fat because she eats too much."

"OK," Andy said, and hurried back to his seat.

"Mom's having a baby," he told Tamika, "and I was writing a list of good baby names."

"You're having a baby!" Tamika said, surprised. "Does that mean I can't move in with you?"

"Of course not," Andy answered. "Mom's not worried about you. She's worried about me. She already told me a baby is not a toy. And, anyway, the baby is not due until May. By then your parents will probably be better and you'll be living with them."

Tamika looked out the window and said softly, "Yeah, probably."

"Let me look at the list," Bruce said.

Andy took the list from his backpack and showed it to Bruce.

"Hey," Bruce said. "These are all boys' names. The baby might be a girl. And you can't call a baby Russell Russell. Your first name can't be the same as your last name."

"Who said it can't?" Andy asked.

"And you can't call a baby Cobalt or Nickel," Bruce said. "Those are metals."

"A name is what you call something, and there are no rules for names," Andy said, and took the notebook from Bruce.

Tamika turned from the window and looked at the list.

"You can name a child just about anything," she said. "But I think Andy's parents will pick the name, not Andy. And the baby might be a girl."

"Yeah, I know," Andy said. "It might be a girl. My parents might find out today what it is. The doctor is giving Mom some kind of a sono-thing. It's like pictures of inside Mom's stomach."

"Moving pictures or still pictures?" Bruce asked.

"I think moving."

"Sound pictures or silent?"

"I don't know."

"Color or black-and-white?"

"Will you please stop asking questions!"

The bus stopped. Bruce looked out the window. "Hey," he said, and quickly grabbed his backpack. "I've got to go. I'll see you tomorrow."

Andy and Tamika got off at the next stop. They crossed the street together. Then, before Tamika went to the Perlmans' house, she asked, "After your parents see those pictures, do you think they'll tell you if it's a boy or a girl?"

"Sure they'll tell me," Andy said. "They just *have* to tell me."

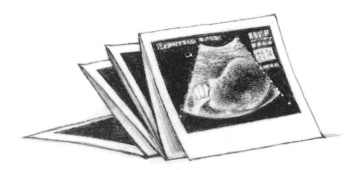

Chapter 2
That Sono-Thing

A ndy was in the basement looking at his gerbils and his pet snake, Slither, when he heard the front door open. He ran upstairs.

"I need to sit," his mother said when she walked into the house.

Mr. Russell was right behind her.

"Did you see pictures of the baby?" Andy asked. "Did it smile? Did he ask for me? Or did *she* smile and ask for me?"

Mrs. Russell sat in the big comfortable chair in the living room. She stretched out her legs, closed her eyes, and sighed.

"This may be too much for me," she said, "working, carrying a baby, and running a household."

"Please," Mr. Russell told Andy. "Let your mother rest."

Andy said, "I won't bother Mom. I'll just listen to her. I'll listen to her stomach."

Andy bent down, put his ear next to his mother's stomach, and asked, "So, how's it going, little baby? Is there any television in there or video games? Any pets? I have lots of gerbils and a snake. Do you want to see them?"

Mrs. Russell opened her eyes and told Andy, "The baby doesn't want to see the gerbils, and right now neither do I."

"Hi, Mom," Rachel said as she walked into the living room. "What did the doctor say?"

Mrs. Russell smiled. "He said the baby and I are just fine."

Andy put his ear close to his mother's stomach again. "Are you a fine boy baby or a fine girl baby?" he asked. Andy listened for a moment.

Then he straightened up and told his parents, "The baby said it wants some of those cherry cheese Danish things they sell at the bakery."

"No," Mrs. Russell said, and smiled. "I think it wants a cup of herbal tea, and so do I. Rachel, could you please make me some?"

Rachel said, "Sure, Mom," and went into the kitchen.

"Herbal tea!" Andy said. "What baby would want anything made from plant leaves?" He pointed at his mother's stomach and asked, "What do you think is in there, a panda?!"

"No," Mrs. Russell told him. "It's not a panda. It's a Russell, a baby Russell. And right now it's just a little bigger than a Danish."

"A cherry cheese Danish?" Andy asked.

"Yes."

Andy looked at his mother's stomach and asked, "Is it really that small?"

"Yes," his mother said again.

Andy put his ear close to his mother's stomach again and listened for a long while. When he didn't hear anything, he straightened up and told his mother, "Well, you're lucky. This baby is quiet, like Rachel. Not noisy, like me."

"I'd be happy," Mrs. Russell said, "if this baby turns out like either one of you."

Rachel called from the kitchen, "The tea is ready."

Mrs. Russell took off her coat, held it out to Andy, and said, "Please hang this up."

"Sure," Andy said, and took the coat. "But first, tell me if you and Dad are happy because the baby is a boy or because it's a girl."

"OK," Mr. Russell said. "We're happy because it's a boy or a girl."

"Yeah, Dad. Very funny. Do you at least know what the baby is?"

Mr. Russell smiled.

"I know that smile," Andy said. "It means you *do* know. And I know I'll find out what the baby is. You can't keep a secret from me!"

Andy went to the hall, got on the stepladder, and hung up his mother's coat. Then he went to the kitchen.

Rachel gave her mother a cup of tea.

"Thank you," Mrs. Russell said, and took a sip.

Mr. Russell watched as his wife slowly drank the tea. Then he said, "It was amazing and so exciting. The doctor showed us a moving picture, a sonogram of the baby." He smiled. "And it's such a beautiful baby."

"It is?" Rachel asked.

"Sure it is," Mrs. Russell said. "All our babies are beautiful."

Andy and Rachel looked at each other.

Andy pointed at his sister and said, "Now don't tell me *she* was ever beautiful!"

"Well," Rachel said. "You never saw me as a baby, but I saw you. And, believe me, you were not a pretty sight."

Here it comes, Andy thought, *her bottle and diaper stories.*

"And you loved to drink milk from a bottle," Rachel said. "I know because I fed you, and you didn't stop until you drank too much and burped it all over me. I even helped Mom change your diaper a few times. And, believe me, when Mom took off that diaper, I saw that nothing about you was ever beautiful!"

"No one told you to look," Andy said.

"And, *wow*—did you smell bad," Rachel said. "You stunk!"

"Well"—Andy pointed at her and shouted, "you stink now!"

"Oh, stop the fighting," Mrs. Russell told them.

Andy thought, *I'll be older than this baby, but I'll respect its privacy. I won't change its diapers.*

Its, Andy thought, *ITS!*

"Hey," Andy said to his father. "You saw this sono-thing. Are we having a boy baby or a girl baby?"

Mr. Russell smiled, but he didn't answer Andy.

"I'm going into the attic," Mr. Russell said, "to work on the new room."

He left the kitchen.

"And I'm going to drink my tea," Mrs. Russell said.

"And no one will answer my question. Is that it?" Andy asked.

Andy stood there for a moment. When no one responded, he said, "Well, I guess that's it."

He decided to follow his father into the attic. Andy thought, *If I ask him when no one else is around, he'll tell me what the baby is.*

Andy went upstairs and into his parents' bedroom. His father was in Mrs. Russell's closet. The trapdoor to the attic was open, and the rope ladder was hanging down, swinging freely. Mr. Russell put his foot on the bottom rung of the ladder and asked Andy, "Are you going to help me?"

Andy looked up at the dark attic. He hated going up there.

"Maybe," Andy said.

"You go first," Mr. Russell told him. "I'll hold the ladder."

Mr. Russell let go of the bottom rung, and Andy put his foot there. He held firmly onto the side ropes and started climbing. After a few steps, he looked back at his father and asked, "Aren't you coming?"

Mr. Russell smiled, put his foot on the first rung, and said, "I'm right behind you."

Andy took a few more steps. He held on to the frame for the trapdoor and pulled himself up.

The attic was dark and cold.

Bats! Andy thought. *This place could be full of bats.* He smiled.

Wouldn't that be great, to have bats as pets? I already know what they eat—bugs, beetles, grasshoppers, and scorpions. That is, if they're vesper bats. They could be fruit bats or maybe vampire bats. Now that would be really great!

Andy imagined Rachel screaming as a vampire bat chased after her.

"Why didn't you turn on the light?" Mr. Russell asked when he climbed into the attic.

He pulled the cord and the light went on. Andy looked around. No bats.

Mr. Russell took a large piece of Sheetrock off the floor and held it against the wooden studs of the attic. He moved it a bit and then said to Andy, "Could you hold this?"

Andy held the Sheetrock, and Mr. Russell hammered it to the studs.

When Mr. Russell was done hammering, Andy asked him, "Why won't you tell me if the baby is a boy or a girl?"

"Your mother and I decided to keep that a secret," Mr. Russell told Andy. "When the baby is born, Mom wants to call people from the hospital and say, 'It's a boy' or, 'It's a girl.' She wants it to be a surprise."

"You can tell me, Dad. I won't tell anyone."

"I know I can, Andy. But we want to surprise you, too." Mr. Russell smiled. "I really wanted to wait. I didn't want to know now what the baby is until it's born. I wanted to be surprised, but when I looked at that sonogram, I knew."

Andy whispered, "Is the baby what we want, Dad? Is it a boy?"

"It's exactly what we want," Mr. Russell said, "a beautiful, healthy child." Then he held up another piece of Sheetrock and said, "Now, let's finish up here."

Mr. Russell was a carpenter, and as he nailed the Sheetrock to the studs, he explained to Andy where he would put the windows, bed, and dresser.

Soon after Andy's parents found out Mrs. Russell was pregnant, they'd decided they needed a new bedroom. Since Rachel was older, the Russells told her she would get it. Mrs. Russell had thought it should be in the basement.

"Hey!" Rachel protested. "I'm not sharing a room with a snake and gerbils."

"And they're not sharing the basement with you," Andy said. "They were there first."

That's when Mr. Russell suggested building a room in the attic.

While Andy was holding a piece of Sheetrock,

he thought about Tamika. *If Dad works fast, she could live up here, in the new room.*

Mr. Russell hammered in a few more nails and then said, "Well, that's it for now. Let's go downstairs."

Andy walked to the trapdoor. He looked at the rope ladder hanging down and touched the side of it with his foot. It started to swing freely. Andy looked at his father.

"I'll go first," Mr. Russell said.

Mr. Russell reached down with his foot and put it on the first rung. When he was in the middle of the ladder, he called to Andy and helped him down.

When they were off the ladder, Mr. Russell whispered to Andy, "Thank you for helping me with the Sheetrock."

"You're welcome," Andy whispered. Then Andy asked, "Dad, why are we whispering?"

Mr. Russell stuck his head out of the closet and pointed at Mrs. Russell. She was lying on her bed with her eyes closed.

"Oh," Andy whispered. Then he told his father, "I'm going downstairs."

Andy went down to the basement. He looked in the snake's tank and said, "Hi, Slither."

Slither didn't seem to notice Andy.

Andy darted his tongue in and out a few times, pretending to be a snake. But, still, Slither didn't respond.

Next to Slither's tank were three gerbil tanks. Andy looked into one of them.

He watched two gerbils run into opposite ends of the plastic tunnel. They ran right into each other. First they both turned. Then one turned again and followed the other gerbil out of the tunnel.

Another gerbil was on the treadmill. It kept running and running, and the treadmill wheel kept spinning and spinning.

"Hey, stop that!" Andy told the gerbil. "You're making me dizzy."

"Psst. Andy," someone whispered.

Andy turned. He and the animals were the only ones in the basement.

Andy looked into the gerbil tank again.

"Psst. Andy. I'm in the cellar." It was Rachel calling to him.

The cellar was what the Russells called their

storage and utility room. The door to it was in the corner of the basement, partially hidden by the side of a bookcase.

"I have to show you something," Rachel whispered. "I found out what the baby is."

Chapter 3
A Dishpan of Tuna

Andy went into the cellar. He looked past the hot water heater, furnace, and water meter, to the corner. Rachel was standing there, next to two boxes of old clothes.

"Look at this," Rachel said. "Look whose is on top."

RACHEL was printed in large letters on the side of one box. ANDY was printed on the side of the other box.

"So what," Andy said. "So what if your box is on top?"

Rachel told him, "Now look inside."

She took the lid off the box. "These are the clothes I outgrew but didn't wear out. Mom started saving them when I was a baby. First she put in my baby things. Then, when I got older and outgrew things, she put them in here, too."

"Rachel," Andy said impatiently. "Get to the point!"

"Just look inside," Rachel said again. "My baby clothes went in first, so they should be at the bottom, right? But they're on top!"

Andy looked in the box. Right on top were a pink baby sleeper and a jumpsuit. And just beneath them were more pink baby things.

"You know what this means, don't you?" Rachel asked. "Mom and Dad were looking through my old stuff, to see what's here for the baby."

Rachel folded her arms and said, "And my box is on top, not yours. That means the last box they were looking through was mine. That must be because they know the baby is a girl."

Andy thought for a moment. *Maybe Rachel is right. Maybe this does mean I'm getting a sister.*

"Hey, wait a minute," Andy said. "Mom and Dad just came home. They looked at this stuff before they saw that sono-thing."

Rachel shook her head. "Mom must have had a feeling the baby would be a girl. Mothers know these things."

Andy looked in the box again. *Two sisters!* He thought. *Well, at least I'll be older than one of them!*

"Thanks for telling me," Andy said to Rachel. "I'll try to prepare myself for another one of you."

Andy returned to the basement. His school-books were on the floor. He decided it was time to do his homework.

Andy opened his history book to chapter four. Twelve pages! *That's a lot of reading,* he thought.

Instead of reading the text, Andy looked at the pictures and read the captions under them. Then he opened his math workbook.

$\frac{1}{4} + \frac{1}{8} = ?$

Who cares? Andy asked himself. But he did the problem anyway.

Adding fractions is such a waste of time, Andy thought. *And Mom thinks math is fun!*

Andy's mother was a math teacher at the local high school.

Andy did some of the homework problems and guessed at the others.

"Andy," Rachel said as she left the cellar, "Mom wants us to make supper. Come upstairs and help."

Andy looked at his sister. There was dust on her shirt and pants. "You're a mess. What were you doing in there so long?" he asked.

Rachel looked down at herself and brushed the dust off. "I was looking at my old clothes," she said. "Some of them are so cute."

Andy closed his books and put them in his backpack. Then he followed Rachel upstairs.

"I'm making salad. You can make the tuna," Rachel said.

"No," Andy told her. "I'll make peanut butter and jelly sandwiches."

Rachel said, "That's kids' stuff. Mom wants salad and tuna."

Andy opened a can of tuna fish and emptied it into a bowl. He added a scoop of mayonnaise and mixed it in. Then he added some parsley flakes.

Rachel looked at the salad.

"You put in too much mayonnaise," she said. "You'd better add another can of tuna."

Andy opened another can of tuna, added it to the salad, and mixed it in.

Rachel looked in the bowl.

"Now it's too dry," she said.

Andy reached for the mayonnaise jar.

"Oh no, you don't," Rachel said. "If you keep adding tuna and then mayonnaise and then more tuna and more mayonnaise, we'll end up with a dishpan full of tuna salad."

Rachel took the jar from Andy and said, "I'll finish this."

After dinner, when no one was looking, Andy put the leftover tuna fish salad in a small plastic container, screwed on the lid, and placed it in his backpack. It was for the kitten at school.

The next morning, at the school bus stop, Rachel told Andy, "I think we should call her Leah. You know, in the Bible, Rachel has a sister named Leah."

"Call the baby Leah? Is it a girl?" the tall Belmont girl asked. She was waiting with her sister for the bus.

Andy looked at Rachel and thought, *You* really *can't keep a secret!*

34

"I don't think so," Andy said. "Leah is not a good name for a vampire bat."

"What?" the short Belmont girl said. "You're getting a vampire bat! They drink blood, don't they?"

"And he has a snake," the tall Belmont told her sister, "and about a hundred mice."

"They're gerbils," Andy said.

"How do you live with all those animals?" the short Belmont asked Rachel.

"They're in the basement and I'm upstairs," Rachel told her.

Andy saw the bus approaching. He turned and looked at the Perlmans' house. The front door was still closed. Tamika was late again.

The bus stopped and the door opened. The Belmonts got right on.

Before Rachel got on, she turned and whispered to Andy, "Thanks for making up that story about the bat. I almost gave away the secret that we're having a sister."

"Who's making up a story?" Andy asked. "I am thinking about getting a vampire bat."

"What?!"

"Let's go! Let's go!" the bus driver, Mr. Cole, called to Rachel and Andy.

Rachel got on. Then, just as Andy put his right foot on the first step, he heard Tamika shout, "Wait! Wait for me!"

Andy waited for Tamika with his right foot on the first step of the bus and his left foot on the street.

"Get on," Mr. Cole told Andy. "I'll wait for her. Don't I always wait for her?"

Andy got on the bus. He said hello to Bruce, who was sitting right behind Mr. Cole. Then he found an empty seat in the back.

Tamika followed Andy onto the bus and sat next to him.

"The Perlman house is full of boxes," Tamika told Andy. "I was helping them pack. You should see all the stuff they're taking to South America."

The bus arrived at school, and as Tamika got off, she told Mr. Cole, "Thank you for waiting for me."

"You're welcome," Mr. Cole said. Then he laughed and added, "You're not punctual, Tamika, but you *are* polite."

"Bye," Andy said to Mr. Cole.

In the front of Andy's classroom was a large box for carnival prizes. Andy looked in it before he went to his seat. The box was empty.

Ms. Roman was wearing a short bright yellow dress.

"Doesn't she look lovely?" Stacy Ann Jackson asked Andy when he sat down.

"Ms. Roman is big and round," Andy said. "With that dress on, she looks like a grapefruit with legs."

"That's stupid," Stacy Ann Jackson said.

You're stupid, Andy thought.

Andy opened his notebook. *Now I have to find a girl's name,* he thought.

Beneath COBALT NICKEL RUSSELL, Andy wrote LEAH RUSSELL.

That's a name for an old lady, Andy thought. *Dawn is a good name for a baby, or Sunny, or Sunrise.* Andy wrote them all in his notebook. *Or Pearl, or Ruby, or Diamond, or Emerald.*

Andy wrote those and other names, too, and occasionally he listened to what Ms. Roman was saying.

When it was time for lunch, Andy took his lunch bag and the plastic container of tuna fish salad from his backpack. He went first to the cafeteria counter and bought a container of milk. Then, as he went to the seat Bruce had saved for him, he walked slowly past the window and looked out. He didn't see the kitten.

"What were you doing in class?" Tamika asked Andy when he sat next to her. "Were you picking names again?"

Andy nodded.

"Boys' names or girls' names?"

"Girls' names."

Tamika patted Andy's hand. "Girls aren't so bad," she said, and smiled. "I'm a girl."

"And anyway," Bruce told him, "when my brother Danny was born, I was so excited that he was a boy. But, you know what, he's just a baby. I can't play catch with him or anything! He just sleeps and cries and fills his diaper. Baby girls do the same thing."

"Yeah," Andy said, "I know. I just thought it would be nice to have a brother."

Andy unwrapped his sandwich and bit into it.

He took out his dessert, a chocolate chip cookie, and ate it quickly. Then he took another big bite of his sandwich.

"Aren't you saving anything for the kitten?" Tamika asked.

"I've got something right here," Andy said, and pointed to the plastic container. "Tuna fish. And this milk is for the kitten, too, if she's out there."

Andy, Tamika, and Bruce finished eating and went outside. They didn't see the kitten, but Andy put the milk and tuna fish in the corner anyway. He took the cover off the plastic container. Then they stood by the fence and waited.

The kitten had been hiding behind the trash cans. She ran to the container and ate the tuna fish quickly. She lapped up the milk. Then she looked over to Andy, Tamika, and Bruce and purred.

Andy smiled.

Tamika said, "She's adorable."

Andy took one small step closer to the kitten. She arched her back and waited. She was about to run, but when Andy didn't move any closer, she stayed where she was.

Andy took a piece of aluminum foil he had saved

from his sandwich and twisted it around one of the links of the fence.

"What are you doing?" Bruce asked.

"I'm marking my spot," Andy explained. "Every day I'll move one step closer until she lets me pet her."

Bruce took one step forward. Tamika did, too. The kitten watched them, but she stayed where she was.

"You know," Bruce said. "Your baby needs a name and this kitten does, too."

The bell rang. Lunchtime was over.

Children hurried off the playground.

"Let's go," Bruce said. "We'll be late to class."

Andy was still watching the kitten.

"You go ahead," Tamika told Bruce. "We'll catch up."

Bruce walked quickly. Andy and Tamika slowly followed him.

"Andy," Tamika said just before they went into the school. "Could you come over later? The Perlmans really like you, and they want to see you before they leave. I think they want to give you something."

Chapter 4
Sylvia

When Andy got off the bus, he told Rachel, "I'm going to the Perlmans'. I'll be home later."

"They've been so busy," Tamika said to Andy as they crossed the street. "Dr. Perlman keeps making lists of things they'll need while they're away, and as soon as they gather everything on the list, he starts another one."

Andy and Tamika were in front of the Perlmans' house. Tamika took a key from her pocket and opened the front door.

"Miriam, I'm home," Tamika called to Mrs. Perlman as she stepped into the house. "Andy is with me."

Andy followed Tamika into the kitchen. Tamika put her backpack on the table and opened the refrigerator. "Do you want something to eat or drink?" she asked Andy.

Andy looked into the refrigerator. On the top shelf were containers of skim milk, apple-raspberry juice, cranberry juice cocktail, prune juice, and carrot juice.

"You drink that stuff?"

Tamika laughed and said, "It's good."

Then she opened the cabinet and offered Andy a raisin bran muffin.

"Yuck!" Andy said.

Tamika laughed again and took a large white box from the cabinet. IN CASE OF EMERGENCY—OPEN WITH CAUTION was printed in large red letters on the lid. She put the box on the kitchen table and opened it. Inside were cans of soda, bags of potato chips and chocolate chip cookies, bubble gum, and a few candy bars.

"Now *this* is food!" Andy said.

Andy took a can of orange soda and a candy

bar. Tamika gave Andy a place mat, a glass with ice, and a napkin. Then she took a muffin and poured a glass of skim milk for herself.

While they were eating, Mrs. Perlman came into the kitchen. She was a short woman with two long braids of gray hair.

"Hello, Tamika. Hello, Andy."

Mrs. Perlman saw the open box, smiled, and said, "I see we had an emergency."

Mrs. Perlman poured a glass of carrot juice for herself and sat next to Tamika. She told Tamika and Andy all about her day and all the trouble she was having deciding what to take to South America.

"We're leaving next week," she said, "and there's still so much to do."

Tamika told Mrs. Perlman about the kitten and Ms. Roman's geography lesson. "She told us about her trip to New Zealand."

"She did?" Andy asked.

Mrs. Perlman looked at Andy.

"Andy dreams a lot," Tamika explained. "Sometimes he doesn't hear everything Ms. Roman says."

Mrs. Perlman smiled and said, "Dreams are fun."

When they finished their snacks, she told Andy, "I'm glad you came. There's something I want to give you. It's in Dr. Perlman's study."

Andy and Tamika followed Mrs. Perlman to a large room lined with book-filled shelves. In front of many of the books were vases, small wooden chests, and framed pictures of the Perlmans in front of statues and monuments in what looked to Andy to be faraway places.

This was Andy's first time in their study. Whenever Andy visited the Perlmans, the door to the study was closed. Andy looked around the room and wondered what Mrs. Perlman would give him.

"Hey, look at that!" Andy said, and pointed to a large brass-and-wood chair. "Can I sit in it?"

"Of course you may," Mrs. Perlman told him. "It's a very old barber's chair."

"It's comfortable," Andy said.

"Dr. Perlman sits in it when he writes his papers and prepares to teach his college classes," Mrs. Perlman told him. "He bought it because he said

he does his best thinking when he's getting his hair cut."

"Look at this," Tamika said. She pointed to a small metal statue of a hunter and a tree. "It's an old bank."

Mrs. Perlman put a dime in a round disk on top of the gun and told Andy, "Now pull back the hunter's arm."

Andy did and the dime shot into the tree.

"That was fun," Andy said. Then he pointed to something that looked like a bouquet of nine flowers with all except one in a straight line. "What's this?" he asked.

"That's a menorah. During Hanukkah we put candles in the flowers."

Andy looked around the room and said, "You sure do have a lot of good stuff in here."

Tamika said, "And a lot of books."

"You can come here and play with Dr. Perlman's toys whenever you want," Mrs. Perlman said. "Now it's time for you to meet Sylvia."

Andy and Tamika followed Mrs. Perlman to a large fish tank on top of a bookcase, just beneath the window. Inside the tank were lots of plants, a castle, and a treasure chest. Bubbles from the filter kept pushing open the lid of the treasure chest. Then Andy saw Sylvia, a large goldfish, swim out of the castle.

"Sylvia may be older than you are," Mrs. Perlman told Andy. "I won her at a carnival many years ago. She was tiny then, but I read somewhere that a goldfish grows to fit the size of its tank. And I think it's true. I bought this tank for Sylvia, and now see how big she is."

Andy looked at all the fun things in Sylvia's tank and thought, *She must love living here.* Then he looked at Tamika and thought, *She must love living here, too.*

"I know you love animals," Mrs. Perlman said, "and if your parents say it's OK, I want you to have Sylvia."

"You do?"

Andy looked in the tank and said, "She'll probably miss her castle and the treasure chest."

"I want you to have everything," Mrs. Perlman said. "I'll give you her food, too, and all her old toys."

"Old toys?" Andy asked.

Tamika told Andy, "Miriam keeps buying things for Sylvia's tank."

Mrs. Perlman took a box from the bookcase beneath the fish tank and showed it to Andy. In it were some rocks, a few toy boats, plastic plants, and a toy deep-sea diver.

"Sylvia can't leave her tank," Mrs. Perlman explained, "and I know it must be boring to stay in the same place all the time, so every few weeks I change things."

Andy looked in the box at Sylvia's toys and said, "Really? I can have all this! Wow! And thanks."

Mrs. Perlman smiled and said, "When we come back from South America, maybe you'll let Dr. Perlman and me visit Sylvia."

"Sure," Andy said. "And you can visit me, too, and the baby Mom's having."

Andy looked in the tank again. He loved to watch the bubbles push open the lid of the treasure chest. Then he told Mrs. Perlman, "I'm going home right now to ask my parents if I can have Sylvia."

Andy hurried home. Rachel was in the kitchen doing her homework.

"Where's Dad? Where's Mom?" Andy asked her.

"Not so loud," Rachel whispered. "They're upstairs."

Andy went to the doorway to his parents' room. Mrs. Russell was sitting by the desk, grading papers. Mr. Russell was sitting on the bed, reading the newspaper.

"Dad," Andy called. "Dad!"

Mr. Russell hurried off the bed. "What is it? What happened?" he asked.

"Nothing happened," Andy answered. "I just want to know if I can have another pet?"

"Another pet! Don't you think a snake and all those gerbils are enough?" Mr. Russell shook his head and said, "There's already enough going on in this house. Next week Tamika is moving in. Soon we're having a baby, and he'll need lots of attention."

"But, Dad," Andy said. "It's only a . . ." Then he stopped, looked up at his father, and asked, "Did you say 'he'?"

"What?"

"When you talked about the baby, you said, *'He'll* need lots of attention.' That means the baby is a boy."

"No, it doesn't," Mr. Russell said quickly. "Now what's this pet you want?"

"But why did you say 'he'?" Andy asked.

"Since when do you listen so carefully to everything I say?" Mr. Russell asked. He sounded annoyed. "Now, what's this pet you want?"

Andy told his father about Mrs. Perlman, Sylvia, the castle, and the treasure chest.

"Rachel said you wanted a bat. I thought that was the new pet you were asking about," Mr. Russell said. "But a goldfish is OK. You can have Sylvia. She won't get out of her tank and scare people. I'll even help you move the tank over here."

"Can we do it now?" Andy asked.

"Sure," his father said.

On their way over to the Perlmans', Andy said, "Dad, I have a great list of boys' names for my new brother."

"Well, make a list of girls' names, too," Mr. Russell told Andy. "I didn't say the baby is a boy."

But Andy was sure he had.

Chapter 5
Questions

Mrs. Perlman took some of the water from the fish tank and put it in a large bowl. She caught Sylvia with a net and put her in the bowl. Andy, Tamika, and Mr. Russell used a plastic pitcher and took turns emptying the tank.

"Good-bye, Sylvia," Mrs. Perlman said. She kissed her fingers and then touched the side of the bowl with them.

Then Andy, Tamika, and Mr. Russell carried the bowl, the tank, and Sylvia's toys next door and down to the Russells' basement. Rachel helped them set up the fish tank next to Slither's.

"Welcome to your new home," Andy said as he tilted the bowl, and Sylvia slid into the tank.

Sylvia looked through the glass at Slither. The snake's forked tongue darted in and out a few times.

"Do you think they'll get along?" Rachel asked.

"Sure, they will," Andy told her. "Slither loves fish." Then he made a sinister look and added, "He loves to *eat* them!"

"That's gross," Rachel said.

"It's not gross," Andy informed his sister. "It's how the food chain works. Strong animals eat weak animals. You eat tuna salad, don't you?"

"But I don't eat goldfish salad," Rachel answered. "And I wouldn't!"

"Anyway, I was joking," Andy said. "Slither only eats tiny minnows. Sylvia is much too big for him."

Mr. Russell plugged in the water filter. He watched the bubbles push open the lid of the treasure chest. Then he went upstairs.

Andy closed the door to the basement behind his father. He quickly went back down the stairs and whispered to Rachel and Tamika, "The baby is a boy."

"No, she's not," Rachel said.

Rachel told Tamika about the clothing box.

"That doesn't mean anything," Andy told them. "Dad was talking about the baby and he said, '*He'll* need lots of attention. *HE'LL!*'"

"That's it!" Rachel exclaimed. "That's it! I'll trap them with pronouns! I'll get Mom and Dad to talk about the baby, and they'll eventually use a pronoun—a *he* or a *she*—and I'll find out what the baby is."

"But I already did that," Andy said. "Dad called the baby a *he*!"

Rachel looked at Andy, shook her head, and said, "Most of the time you don't hear what Dad says, or Mom, or your teacher, or anyone."

Andy looked at Tamika.

She just shrugged.

"And when you do hear something," Rachel continued, "half the time you get it wrong."

Rachel told Tamika, "The first day of kindergarten, his teacher asked his name and he said, 'Peanut butter!' He thought she asked what he had for lunch."

"Really?" Tamika asked.

Rachel nodded. "The teacher told Mom and Dad to have his hearing tested and they did."

"And my hearing was fine," Andy said. "And I heard Dad call the baby *he*!"

"I don't think so," Rachel said, and shook her head. "Tomorrow morning I'll find out for sure if the baby is a girl or a boy."

The next morning Andy was down early for breakfast. He quietly ate his cereal and listened as Rachel tried to get Mrs. Russell to talk about the baby.

"Is the baby kicking?" Rachel asked.

"No."

"Does it kick a lot?"

"Sometimes. Mostly it just swims in amniotic fluid."

"Swims?" Andy asked, surprised.

Mrs. Russell nodded.

Andy was impressed. *I didn't learn to swim until I was seven,* he thought.

Andy watched his mother eat cottage cheese and toast. He imagined the food dropping into a large swimming pool in her stomach, and the baby sitting by the pool, reading a magazine. He imagined the baby seeing the food, jumping off a diving board, and swimming to it.

"Hey, Mom?" Andy asked. "Does the baby really swim? And do you think it likes wet toast?"

Mrs. Russell finished chewing and said, "Sure . . ." She started to say something and stopped herself. "Sure," she said very slowly. "The baby loves it."

Mrs. Russell took another bite of toast.

I almost got her, Andy thought.

All during the bus ride to school, Andy thought of more questions he could ask to trick his mother into using a pronoun.

Does it hurt when it kicks?

When the baby yawns, do you burp?

Does the baby pay attention when you teach math, or does it dream in class like I do?

In class, before he went to his seat, Andy looked in the prize box. He saw an old football, a torn comic book, and a small teddy bear.

Who wants that stuff? Andy wondered. *It's junk, not prizes!*

There were a few jars on Ms. Roman's desk.

"Hey, Ms. Roman," Andy said. "There are no holes in the lids. How will the gerbils breathe?"

"When we get some more jars," she told him, "you can take them all to the wood shop and get them ready for the gerbils."

Andy sat in his seat and opened his notebook. He looked at his list of names. Then he tried to listen to Ms. Roman.

She taught a geography lesson first. Then she gave the class the test on fractions.

Andy looked at the first question: *How would three people share a whole pizza pie—eight slices?*

What a dumb question! Andy thought. *That's more than two slices each! Who eats that much?*

Andy did the problem anyway.

There were problems with apples, apple pies, licorice, and chocolate cakes. By the time Andy finished the test, he was hungry.

Andy was checking his answers when the bell rang. It was time for lunch.

After Ms. Roman collected the tests, Stacy Ann Jackson turned and told Andy, "That test was fun. I think I got every question right."

Andy reached under his seat for his lunch.

Stacy Ann Jackson stood, looked down at Andy, and said again, "I think I got every question right."

"I heard you the first time," Andy said as he

walked past her. "You think you're smarter than I am, and maybe you are. But I don't care."

When Andy got to the cafeteria, he dropped his lunch bag on the table and told Tamika and Bruce, "My stomach is confused. That test made me hungry, and Stacy Ann Jackson made me want to barf."

"Eat slowly," Tamika suggested.

"She told me, 'I think I got every question right.' Like *I* care," Andy said, really annoyed.

Andy took the cookie out of his lunch bag and bit into it.

"Don't let her upset you," Bruce said. "When we're done, we'll go outside and see Fluffy."

"And see who?" Andy asked.

"The kitten," Bruce answered. "I named her Fluffy."

Andy pointed his half-eaten cookie at Bruce. "Fluffy!" Andy said. "What do you think she is— a pillow?!"

Bruce didn't respond.

"I found her," Andy said. "I feed her and *I'll* name her."

Andy bit into his cookie again.

Fluffy! Andy thought. *What kind of a name is that?!*

Andy thought of all the great names he had written in his notebook for the baby and wondered if one would be good for the kitten.

Grover? Dawn? Sunrise?

Andy finished the cookie and then took the top piece of bread off his sandwich and ate it. He saved the bottom piece, with the cream cheese, for the kitten.

Pearl? Ruby? Emerald?

Andy couldn't decide what to name the kitten.

"I'm buying some milk," Andy told Tamika and Bruce. "Then let's go outside."

On his way to the cafeteria counter, Andy walked slowly past the windows. He looked for the kitten, but he didn't see her. When he came back to the table, Tamika and Bruce had finished eating.

When they were on the playground, Tamika and Bruce stood by the fence. Andy went to the corner of the playground. He opened the milk container and put it on the ground. He put the bread, with the cream cheese facing up, next to the milk. Then he joined Tamika and Bruce.

The kitten had been hiding behind the trash cans again. She ran to the milk.

Andy looked behind him, at the fence. He was standing right by his twisted piece of aluminum foil. Andy took one step closer to the kitten and watched her lap up the milk.

"She's so pretty," Tamika said. "In the sunlight, her fur looks almost silver."

"Silver," Andy said. "I can call her Silver."

Then he remembered his list of names and said, "But I won't. Because I'm calling her Cobalt."

Andy was pleased with the name.

"Cobalt is shiny and silver colored," Andy explained, "just like she is."

Bruce said, "And cobalt is magnetic."

Andy and Tamika looked at him.

"The metal is magnetic," Bruce explained, "not the kitten."

At the end of the lunch period, Andy walked slowly past Cobalt.

"Bye, Cobalt," Andy said to her. "I'll see you tomorrow.

"Meow," Cobalt answered.

Chapter 6
Gerbil Contract

The carnival is Monday," Ms. Roman told the class after lunch. "We still need more prizes and more jars."

Andy raised his hand.

"Yes, Andrew."

"When should I bring in the gerbils? And how many?"

"Tomorrow is Friday. We'll count the jars we have then, and on Monday you can bring in one gerbil for each jar."

"I have one," Stacy Ann Jackson said. "I have a jar filled with orange juice. I'll finish it tonight and be fortified with vitamin C."

"Thank you," Ms. Roman said.

"I also have volume L of an encyclopedia," Stacy Ann Jackson continued, "with articles on lakes and light and London and Abraham Lincoln. My mom bought it at the supermarket, and I already read it. I can bring that in, too, for a prize."

"Thank you," Ms. Roman said again.

L, Andy thought. *Before you bring it in, look up "loony." Maybe you're mentioned.*

Ms. Roman gave a science lesson about magnetic fields. She asked Bruce to hold a sheet of paper parallel to the ground. Then with one hand she held a magnet under it and with the other she sprinkled on iron filings.

"Gently shake the paper," she told Bruce.

Bruce shook the paper.

"Hey," he said when he looked down at the paper, "they're in two circles."

Ms. Roman had the children come up one at a time to look at the pattern of the magnetic fields.

"Andy," Bruce whispered when Andy looked at

the iron filings, "could you save a gerbil for me? I'm not sure I can win one."

"Sure," Andy told him.

When Andy returned to his seat, he thought about Bruce and the gerbils and the children at the carnival who might win them as prizes.

"I know! I know!" Stacy Ann Jackson called out.

Ms. Roman had asked a question, and Stacy Ann Jackson wanted to answer it.

What if she *wins a gerbil!* Andy shuddered. *Anyone can win one.*

Next, Ms. Roman gave a geography lesson about latitude, longitude, the equator, and the prime meridian. But Andy wasn't interested. He was worried about his gerbils.

I'll write a contract, he decided. *Everyone who wins a gerbil will have to sign it.*

Andy opened his notebook. Beneath his list of girls' names he wrote: I AGREE TO TAKE GOOD CARE OF MY GERBIL, TO GIVE IT FOOD AND WATER. He thought about Sylvia and added, I ALSO AGREE TO GET A NICE TANK FOR IT TO LIVE IN, TO BUY IT TOYS, AND TO LOVE IT.

"Andrew," Ms. Roman said.

Andy looked up.

"I see you're taking notes. That's very good."

Bruce quickly opened his notebook and told Ms. Roman, "I'm taking notes, too."

Andy thought, *Bruce might name his gerbil Fluffy!*

I ALSO AGREE, Andy added to his contract, NOT TO CALL MY GERBIL FLUFFY OR ANY OTHER STUPID NAME.

Ms. Roman ended the day with silent reading. Andy opened a book and pretended to read it, but he was really thinking about his gerbils. He wondered if he should add any more clauses to the contract.

RRRR!

The bell rang.

It was time to go home.

As Andy gathered his books and put them in his backpack, Stacy Ann Jackson turned and told him, "I have a very good memory. I don't have to take notes."

"That's because you're *so* smart," Andy said sarcastically. Then he zipped his backpack and left the classroom.

On the bus Tamika said, "In five days the Perlmans are leaving."

"And then you move in with us," Andy said.

Tamika looked out the window. She was quiet for a while.

"Could I pick the gerbil you give me?" Bruce asked Andy.

"Only if you promise not to call it Fluffy."

Bruce said, "I promise."

Bruce thought for a moment and said, "I'll call it Ginger."

Andy shook his head.

"Pepper?"

"Yeah, Pepper is a good name."

Tamika turned from the window. There were tears in her eyes.

"First my parents had that accident," Tamika said, trying to keep from crying. "And I was so scared for them. And when I knew they would get better, I was scared for me. I didn't know where I would live until they were well enough to come home."

Bruce gently put his hand on Tamika's.

"Then the Perlmans became my foster parents, and I really love them. Now they're leaving."

"But you're moving in with us," Andy said.

Tamika smiled a little and told him, "I know. And that will be great. But I'll still really miss the Perlmans."

"Hey, Bruce!" Mr. Cole, the bus driver called. "Are you getting off?"

"Yes," Bruce said, and grabbed his backpack.

"I'll see you tomorrow," he told Andy and Tamika. Then he hurried off the bus.

Andy, Tamika, Rachel, and the Belmont girls got off at the next stop.

"Bye," Andy said to Tamika after they had crossed the street.

He knew he should have told her something comforting about the Perlmans going away. But he didn't know what to say.

When Andy got in the house, he went right to the basement. He sprinkled some goldfish flakes into Sylvia's tank and watched her swim to the top and eat.

He tapped on Slither's tank and said, "Hi."

Slither stuck its forked tongue out at Andy. Andy stuck *his* rounded tongue out at Slither.

Andy looked into each of the three gerbil tanks

and watched them for a few minutes. Then he turned on the computer.

He opened the design program and chose a fancy border like the one on his mother's college diploma. Then, in large bold letters, he typed: GERBIL CONTRACT. Beneath that, in smaller letters, he copied the contract he had written in class. Then he typed a line and wrote SIGN HERE.

Andy clicked PRINT FULL DOCUMENT.

Maybe there'll be enough jars for all of my gerbils, Andy thought.

Andy typed in 50 COPIES and clicked again.

Andy watched the printer grab one sheet of paper after another and the printed contracts drop into the tray.

The door to the basement opened.

"Hey, Andy!" Rachel called from the top of the stairs. "What are you doing?"

"Printing contracts."

"What?" Rachel asked, and came down the stairs.

Andy showed her one of the contracts.

"You're weird," she said. "I wouldn't sign this."

"And you wouldn't take good care of a gerbil," Andy told her.

"You're right," Rachel admitted.

She looked in the fish tank. While she watched Sylvia swim in and out of the castle, Andy told her what Tamika had said about the Perlmans.

Rachel thought about that. "You know what we should do?" she said. "We should print some signs and banners welcoming Tamika. We should try to make her feel real good about living with us."

"And we should bake a cake," Andy suggested.

"With icing and words on it," Rachel added.

"And we should have cookies," Andy said, "and candies, and balloons, and presents."

Rachel said, "First, let's do the signs and banners."

Rachel pulled over a chair and sat down. Andy looked at the printer. It had stopped grabbing sheets of paper and printing contracts. He moved the computer mouse, opened a file on the menu, and clicked that he wanted to make a sign.

They made signs that said WELCOME TAMIKA!, OUR HOME IS TAMIKA'S HOME!, TAMIKA'S NEW HOME, SWEET HOME!, and a banner that said THE RUSSELL FAMILY LOVES TAMIKA ANDERSON!

Andy printed out several large pictures of balloons.

They were about to hang the signs, the banner, and the balloon pictures when Mr. and Mrs. Russell came home.

"What's all this?" Mrs. Russell asked.

Andy told his parents what Tamika had said about being scared and how she would miss the Perlmans.

"She'll probably come here before Tuesday, to visit or bring her things," Mrs. Russell said. "So we should wait to hang the signs. They should be a surprise to welcome her when she moves in."

"We want to bake a cake, too," Rachel said.

"And cookies," Andy added.

"Let's have dinner first," Mr. Russell said. "Then we can all bake together."

"I have a better idea," Mrs. Russell told them. "First, let's eat. Then we can decide what to bake. I'll make a list of the ingredients we'll need, and I'll pick them up tomorrow. And we can bake on Sunday or Monday. Let's welcome Tamika on Tuesday with a freshly baked cake and cookies, not stale ones."

Chapter 7
In Case of Emergency

The next morning there were nineteen large jars in the box on the floor behind Ms. Roman's desk. Andy unscrewed the lids, filled his pockets with them, and took them to the wood shop. The teacher there helped Andy poke holes in each of them with a hammer and an awl.

When he got back to class, Andy showed Ms. Roman the holes in the lids and told her, "Now the gerbils will be able to breathe."

"That's good," Ms. Roman said. "Just put the lids on the jars and return to your seat."

Andy took a lid from his shirt pocket and a jar from the box. He tried to screw on the lid, but it didn't fit.

Andy tried the lid on another jar. It didn't fit on that one, either.

He looked at the lid and asked it, "You just want to cause trouble, don't you?"

The lid didn't answer.

Andy sat on the floor. He took another lid from his pants pocket and tried it on the two jars. It didn't fit either of them.

"You lids are all a bunch of troublemakers!"

Ms. Roman was writing on the chalkboard. She looked down and said, "Andrew, please do that quietly."

"Shh," Andy whispered to the jar lids.

He took the jars out of the box and lined them up on the floor under Ms. Roman's desk. Then he whispered to a lid, "Now, I'll find you a mate."

He tried it on what looked to him like a large jelly jar and asked, "Do you like this one?"

The lid didn't fit.

"Too fat for you?" Andy asked.

He tried the lid on another jar.

It didn't fit.

"And now you think this one is too thin," Andy asked. "You're a picky lid, aren't you?"

Andy crawled under the desk and tried the lid on one jar after another until he finally found its mate.

"Andrew," Ms. Roman said, "just what are you doing under there?"

Andy poked his head out from under the desk and said, "I'm finding husbands and wives for lonely lids and jars."

"What?"

"I'm matching the lids to the jars."

"Please, do it quietly," Ms. Roman told him.

"Shh," Andy whispered, and crawled under the desk again. He stayed there through most of the geography lesson, until all the lids were on.

Just after Andy got to his seat and opened his geography book, Ms. Roman took a pile of papers from her book bag and said, "Now, I'll return your math tests."

Andy closed his book.

Ms. Roman zigzagged around the room, handing out the tests. When Bruce got his, he smiled and held it up for Andy to see: 74.

For Bruce, that was a good grade.

When Tamika got her test, she looked at it, but she didn't hold it up. She never showed Andy her tests. She thought they were private. But Andy knew she always got good grades.

Ms. Roman gave Stacy Ann Jackson her test.

"YES!" Stacy Ann Jackson called out.

She turned and showed it to Andy: 100.

Andy shook his head and told Stacy Ann, "I'm disappointed in you. You're not showing any improvement. That's what you got on the last test."

"I'm not?" she asked.

She looked at her test and suddenly declared, "Of course I'm not. One hundred is the best grade I can get!"

Andy laughed. He loved to tease Stacy Ann.

Where is mine? Andy wondered.

Andy's was one of the last tests Ms. Roman returned.

He got an 82.

His math grades were usually in the eighties. Andy was satisfied.

Ms. Roman went over the test, but Andy wasn't interested. He hoped he never saw another fraction and never had to share eight slices of pizza with two other people.

During lunch period, Andy bought a container of milk for Cobalt. He stood by the fence with Tamika and Bruce and watched Cobalt lap up the milk.

When she had finished, Andy took an easy-open can of tuna fish and a plastic fork from his pocket. He pulled off the top of the can and scooped out a forkful of tuna. He slowly took two steps closer to Cobalt, crouched, and held the fork out to her.

Cobalt ran to Andy and he fed her the entire can.

"Does it taste good? Does it?" Andy asked her.

Cobalt looked at Andy, tilted her head to one side, and purred.

A ball bounced nearby. Cobalt's tail went up. Her back arched. Then she turned and ran behind the trash cans.

Two boys ran toward the ball.

Andy grabbed it and yelled, "Watch where you're playing!" And he threw the ball against the fence.

"Hey!" the boys yelled.

Andy made what he hoped was a mean-looking face. The boys turned and ran after the ball.

Andy picked up the empty milk container and rejoined Tamika and Bruce.

"Did you see that?" Andy asked. "Just when Cobalt and I were getting acquainted, those boys scared her away."

Andy waited. He hoped Cobalt would come out from behind the trash cans. But she didn't.

"I'm worried about her," Andy said. "It's Friday. I won't be here tomorrow. What will she eat?"

"She'll have what she ate last weekend, before you found her," Tamika told him.

RRRR!

The lunch period ended. Andy threw away the empty milk container and tuna fish can and found a half-eaten bologna sandwich on top of the trash. He put it on the ground. On his way inside, he turned and saw Cobalt nibble the meat.

"That's what she eats when you're not here," Bruce said. "Trash."

In the afternoon Ms. Roman talked about the carnival. It would be in the gym. Tamika, Bruce, and Nicole Adams would take care of the beanbag toss game. There would be a target on the floor behind the table, and children would toss bean-bags and try to get them to land in the bull's-eye.

There would be other games, too. And Andy would help Ms. Roman at the prize table.

Ms. Roman reminded everyone what he or she had volunteered to bring in for the carnival. She also asked for more prizes.

"I can print FREE GAME coupons on my computer," Bruce suggested. "We can give those out as prizes."

"And I can print WINNER certificates," Stacy Ann Jackson said.

"Those are excellent ideas," Ms. Roman told them.

The class made crepe-paper vests and bow ties to wear, so children would know who was running the games. Andy made a long green vest. It reached his knees.

"That looks like a dress," Tamika told him. "Do you want me to cut it?"

"Yeah," Andy said.

Tamika took a pair of scissors from Ms. Roman's desk. She cut the paper so the vest bottom had two points and reached just below Andy's waist.

"Do you want it to look really good?" Tamika asked.

"Sure," Andy answered.

Tamika cut three small round circles out of white crepe paper and pasted them in a row, down the center of the vest.

"Hey, buttons!" Andy said.

"I'm not done," Tamika told him.

She cut a small white rectangle of paper. Then she cut three small triangles out of the top of it and pasted what was left of the rectangle on the front left side of the vest.

"Hey, a pocket with a handkerchief!" Andy said.

He went to Ms. Roman's closet and looked in her mirror.

"This looks really good," he told Tamika. "Thank you."

When the bell rang and the school day ended, Andy carefully folded his vest and put it in his desk.

On the bus Tamika told Andy and Bruce, "The Perlmans are almost all packed. They called a car service to take them to the airport Tuesday afternoon."

"Can you go with them to the airport?" Bruce asked.

Tamika wiped her eyes with the back of her hand and said, "No. The car service won't wait and bring me back to the house."

Andy looked at Tamika. She was about to cry.

"I'll ask my dad if he can take them," Andy told her. "If he does, after he drives them to the airport, he'll come back to our house. That way, you can go along."

"That would be great," Tamika said. "Thank you."

That evening, when Mrs. Russell came home, she told Andy and Rachel, "Please help your father."

Mr. Russell was outside, taking groceries out of the car trunk.

"What is all this stuff?" Andy asked.

"Just *help*!" Rachel told him.

Andy looked into the bags. He picked one with a box of sugared cereal and cake mixes.

When all the bags were in the house, Andy and Rachel helped their parents empty them.

"Where's the tuna fish?" Andy asked.

"I didn't know we needed any," Mr. Russell said.

"We do," Andy told him. "There's a kitten at school and I'm feeding it."

"You're not feeding it tuna fish!" Mr. Russell said really loud. "And I hope you're not planning to bring it home. We have enough animals living in this house."

"Cobalt lives at school," Andy told his father. "I won't bring her home. I just want to feed her."

"Tuna fish is expensive," Mr. Russell said. "I buy it for us, not for a stray cat."

"But she's hungry," Andy said. There were tears in his eyes. "She needs to eat."

Mr. Russell looked at Andy, touched his cheek, and said softly, "All right, if you promise not to bring it home, tomorrow or Sunday I'll go shopping again and buy a few cans of cat food."

"Thanks, Dad."

In the bags were mixes for a chocolate cake and sugar cookies, a container of ready-made icing, and a tube of cake-decorating gel. There were also a container of baby powder, baby wipes, diapers, and tubes of cream.

Rachel looked at Andy, smiled, and then asked Mr. Russell, "Are these diapers for the baby?"

"Yes, I know it's really early to be buying these things, but seeing the sonogram got me excited. Buying all this was fun. It reminded me of when the two of you were babies."

Andy knew Rachel was trying to find out if the baby was a boy or a girl. She hoped her dad would refer to the baby as either "he" or "she."

"Are you sure you bought enough?"

"Yes. I'll buy more after . . ." Andy was sure he was about to say "he."

"I'll buy more after," Mr. Russell said very deliberately, "the *baby* is born."

Andy told his father, "You almost said *he*."

"No," Rachel told her father. "You almost said *she*."

Mr. Russell smiled.

When the groceries were put away, Andy asked his father if he could drive the Perlmans to the airport.

"Tamika wants to go along, to say good-bye, and she can't if they go with a car service."

"Sure," Mr. Russell said. "And if there's room, you can come along, too."

Andy went right over to the Perlmans. He rang the bell and waited to tell Tamika the good news.

Dr. Perlman answered the door. There were three hats on his head, two neckties draped over his shoulder, and he was holding a hanger with two shirts on it.

"Hello, Andy."

Andy tried not to laugh, but he couldn't help it.

Dr. Perlman's eyes rolled up.

"Is it the hats?" he asked. "Do they look funny?"

Andy nodded.

"Come in," Dr. Perlman said.

Andy followed him into the house. There were several open suitcases in the living room. Dr. Perlman put the shirts and neckties in one of the suitcases. Then he took off all three hats.

"We'll be in the sun a lot," Dr. Perlman told Andy. "And if I don't wear a hat, I'll get this all burned." He bent down and showed Andy the big round bald spot in the center of his head.

Mrs. Perlman and Tamika came out of the kitchen and greeted Andy. Then Mrs. Perlman asked her husband, "Were you showing off your bald spot?"

Dr. Perlman nodded.

Mrs. Perlman told Andy, "He's so proud of it."
Dr. Perlman smiled.

"Oh," Mrs. Perlman said to Andy, "I have something else to give you." She hurried back to the kitchen.

"Wait," Andy said. He told the Perlmans that his father could take them all to the airport.

"That's so great," Tamika said.

"We have a lot of luggage," Dr. Perlman said. "It won't all fit in the trunk."

"There's a rack on the roof of the car," Andy told him.

"That's nice of your father," Mrs. Perlman said. "Now, you wait here."

Mrs. Perlman hurried into the kitchen and then came back carrying the large white IN CASE OF EMERGENCY—OPEN WITH CAUTION box.

"This is for you," she said, and gave the box to Andy.

Andy peeked into the box. He wanted to be sure it had the good stuff in it, not muffins and carrot juice. It did.

"Thanks," he said. "Thanks a lot."

Andy stayed awhile. He tried to help the Perlmans pack, but there was very little for him to do, so he went home. On his way, he considered putting the IN CASE OF EMERGENCY box in the kitchen cabinet. *But this is my stuff,* he thought. He put the box in his closet and hid it in the corner, behind his bathrobe.

Sunday afternoon Andy was in the basement, playing with Slither, when Rachel opened the door and called down, "Let's bake the cookies now for Tamika."

Andy took Slither off his shoulder and put him back in the tank.

"Bye, old boy," he said to the snake as he slid the screen onto the top of the tank.

"Wash your hands," Rachel told Andy when he came into the kitchen. "With soap!"

Andy washed his hands.

Rachel gave him a bowl, a mixing spoon, and the box of sugar cookie mix. Then she turned on the oven, set the temperature, and took out the cookie sheets.

Andy opened the box of cookie mix and poured the dry ingredients into the bowl. Then he scooped out a spoonful of powder and ate it.

"What are you doing?" Rachel shouted. "Now the whole mix recipe is off."

Andy took another spoonful of powder, tilted his head back, opened his mouth, and sprinkled the mix in.

Rachel pushed him away from the bowl.

"You're ruining the mix," she said, and pointed to the back of the box. "Look at this. We're supposed to add half a cup of oil and one egg to one package of mix. But we don't have one package of mix anymore! You ate some of it."

"Oh, you make such a big deal out of everything," Andy told her. "The cookies will be just fine."

Andy added the oil and the egg. He stirred the mix. He and Rachel each made balls of cookie dough with a spoon and dropped them onto a cookie sheet. Rachel's cookie dough balls were in neat rows, and each was about the same size.

Andy molded his into the shapes of animals. One was long, thin, and twisted.

"This one is a snake," he told Rachel.

Several were tiny.

"These are ants," Andy said.

One was enormous.

"This one is a bear," Andy said.

Rachel shook her head in disbelief and put both sheets in the oven.

While the cookies were baking, Andy and Rachel prepared the chocolate cake mix.

The timer rang.

Just as Rachel was taking the cookies out of the oven, Mr. Russell came into the kitchen.

"I was in the attic and I smelled something good," he said. He looked at Andy's cookie sheet and said, "These tiny ones are burned, and this big one isn't completely baked."

Mr. Russell lifted off the small, burned cookies with a spatula. He put the big one back in the oven.

"Those are Andy's," Rachel said. "Look at mine."

"Yours look good," Mr. Russell said. He scraped the burnt bottom off one of Andy's and ate it. "And Andy's taste good," he said.

Mr. Russell helped them bake the cake and put icing on it. With the tube of decorating gel, Andy wrote WECOME TAMIKA! on top of the cake. Mr.

Russell added an L and changed WECOME to WEL-COME.

Mr. Russell put the cake in the refrigerator and the cookies in a tin. Then he helped Andy and Rachel clean the kitchen.

"Don't eat any of my cookies," Rachel told Andy when they were done. "They're for Tamika."

"And don't you eat any of mine," Andy told her, "especially not the bear."

"Don't worry," Rachel said as she washed her hands. "I won't."

Andy took one of his tiny ant cookies from the tin and ate it.

Yuck, he thought. *This tastes like charcoal.*

He waited for Rachel to leave the kitchen. Then he spit what was left of his cookie into the garbage.

"No good?" Mr. Russell asked.

"No good," Andy answered.

"Rachel follows directions and recipes," Mr. Russell told Andy. "Sometimes that's a good idea."

"Yeah, I guess," Andy said.

Mr. Russell smiled. "How would you like to

come to the attic and help me?" he asked. "I'm about to cut a hole in the roof."

"You are?"

"It's for the window of the new room."

Cutting a hole in the roof sounded like fun, but Andy had to prepare for tomorrow's carnival.

Andy shook his head and said, "Sorry, Dad. I have to pick the nineteen unfortunate gerbils who will spend a day in school with me and Ms. Roman."

Chapter 8
Global Warming

The next morning at the bus stop, along with his backpack, Andy had a shopping bag filled with gerbil food and wood chips and his father's old metal toolbox. The toolbox had small holes on the side for ventilation, which was why Andy picked it. Inside it were nineteen gerbils.

The short Belmont girl leaned over and looked in the shopping bag. Then she looked at the toolbox.

"What's in there?" she whispered to Rachel.

"Gerbils," Rachel whispered back.

The short Belmont girl pointed to the box and shouted, *"Gerbils? Rodents!* That's what's in that box!"

"You're not bringing those mice on our bus," the tall Belmont girl told Andy.

Andy bent down and reached for the latch and said, "If I can't take them on the bus, they'll just have to walk to school."

Andy started to open the latch.

"No!" the short Belmont shouted. "Don't open it!"

The bus was approaching. Andy turned and looked at the Perlman house. The door was still closed.

The bus stopped and the bus door opened.

The short Belmont girl got on, pointed to Andy, and told Mr. Cole, "He's got mice in that box. You're not going to let him get on with them, are you?"

"Just sit down," Mr. Cole told her.

The tall Belmont girl followed her sister onto the bus and asked, "What if they get loose?"

Mr. Cole assured her, "They won't get loose."

"I hope not," the tall Belmont girl said, and found a seat in the middle of the bus.

Rachel got on. Then Andy put his right foot on the first step and turned to look again at the Perlman house. The door was still closed.

"Let's go!" Mr. Cole told Andy. "Let's go!"

Andy got on and sat next to Bruce, near the front of the bus.

"Where's Tamika?" Mr. Cole asked Andy.

"I don't know."

Mr. Cole waited for a moment and watched the front of the Perlman house.

Then he turned and told Andy, "I'm sorry. It's late. I've got to get going."

Mr. Cole pulled a lever and the door to the bus closed. He drove slowly past the Perlmans' house. He stopped the bus and waited another moment. Then he drove on to school.

When Andy went into class, he pointed to the toolbox and told Ms. Roman, "I have the gerbils. They're in here."

"Can they stay in there until this afternoon?" she asked.

"I think so," Andy answered. "If I open it sometimes, and let in some extra air."

"Fine," Ms. Roman said. "Just keep it by your seat and be careful."

Andy went to his seat. He put his backpack under his desk and the shopping bag and toolbox next to it.

Stacy Ann Jackson turned around and whispered, "What's in the box?"

"Nineteen crawling, scratching, twitching gerbils," Andy told her.

"That's nice," Stacy Ann Jackson said.

It is? Andy asked himself. *I thought she'd be scared.*

In the middle of the math lesson, Tamika entered the room. She gave Ms. Roman a note and then walked to her seat. After she sat down, she turned and waved to Andy.

"Multiplying with fractions is really like division," Ms. Roman said. "The answer you get is smaller than the number you start with."

Multiplication that's like division! Andy thought. *This stuff is too confusing!*

He tapped his foot on the toolbox and heard

the gerbils move. *They must need some air,* Andy thought. He bent down and unhooked the latch.

Andy opened the box just a crack, and a gerbil's tail stuck out. Andy quickly pushed the gerbil's tail back in and closed the box.

Ms. Roman went on with the lesson. And Andy thought about the gerbils, Tamika and the Perlmans, Cobalt, and the baby. He still wondered if it was a boy or a girl.

At lunchtime Andy took the gerbils to the cafeteria.

He bought a container of milk for Cobalt. Then, when he got to the table, he asked Tamika, "Why were you late?"

"Last night," she said, "we stayed up past midnight. We were talking and singing the Perlmans' favorite old songs. And this morning we were all too tired to get up."

"What did you talk about?" Andy asked.

"The Perlmans talked about when they were young and about their travels. I talked about my parents, school, and my friends."

Bruce asked, "Did you talk about me?"

"Of course I did. I said you were one of my best friends."

Bruce smiled.

They ate quietly for a while. Then, when Andy had finished his lunch, he put the toolbox on the table and opened the top a crack. A gerbil stuck its nose out.

"Let me look in. Let me pick mine," Bruce said, and reached to open the top more.

Andy quickly pushed the gerbil's nose back in, closed the toolbox, and warned Bruce, "Don't touch this! We can't let them out!"

Bruce pulled back his hand.

When they went outside, Andy put the toolbox on the ground. Then he opened the container of milk and put it down.

Cobalt peeked out from behind a trash can and looked at Andy, Tamika, and Bruce.

Andy took a plastic fork from his shirt pocket. Then he reached into his pants pocket and took out one of the cans of cat food his father had bought. He pulled off the top and said, "Look what I have for you."

Cobalt ran to him and Andy fed her.

When she was finished eating, Cobalt sniffed the toolbox.

"She smells the gerbils," Tamika whispered.

Bruce laughed. "You didn't like the names I picked out for the gerbil you're giving me, but I know what Cobalt would call them."

"What?" Andy asked.

"Breakfast, Lunch, and Dinner."

"Very funny," Andy said. "Very funny."

When they went back to class, Ms. Roman gave a short lesson on current events. She read from an article about a storm in the Caribbean Sea and about the dangers of global warming.

"Who knows what global warming is?" Ms. Roman asked.

Nicole Adams raised her hand and shouted, "I do! I do!"

"Yes, Nicole?"

"A globe is a map that's pasted onto something round," Nicole Adams said, "and if it gets warm, the paste will melt and the map will fall off."

Andy knew that global warming had nothing to do with paste. He had seen a program at the

science museum about global warming and how it might affect endangered animal species.

"I'm sorry, Nicole, but that's not right," Ms. Roman said. "Stacy Ann, could you please tell us about global warming."

"Well," Stacy Ann said slowly, "global warming . . ." She paused. "Global warming," she said again slowly, and looked up at the ceiling.

Ms. Roman and the class waited. But Stacy Ann Jackson couldn't answer the question.

Andy raised his hand.

"Yes, Andrew?"

"The temperature of the earth keeps going up," Andy said. "And that's making the level of the oceans rise, and there are more floods and that's bad."

Ms. Roman smiled and said, "Thank you, Andrew."

After the lesson Ms. Roman told the class to take their vests and the boxes filled with things for the carnival and follow her to the gym.

"You don't know everything," Andy told Stacy Ann Jackson when they were in the hall. "And I'm not stupid."

Stacy Ann Jackson told Andy, "I never said you

were stupid. And I don't think you are. I just like to talk to you. That's what friends do. They talk."

There were tears in her eyes.

Friends? Andy thought. *Who said we were friends?*

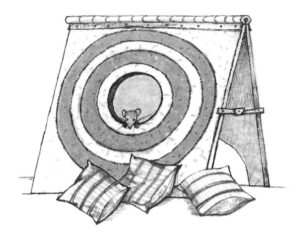

Chapter 9
I'll Get You!

Mr. Dexter, the custodian, was in the gym to help the fourth-grade classes set up the carnival.

"We'll have one table here, by the entrance," Ms. Roman told Mr. Dexter, "to sell the game tickets, six tables on each side for the games, and two at the other end for the prizes."

"I'll take care of it," Mr. Dexter said.

He asked Bruce and two boys from the other

fourth-grade class to help him, and they quickly had all the tables in place.

"Now," Ms. Roman told the children, "set up your games. And, Andrew, I'll help you set up the prize table."

Mr. Williams, the other fourth-grade teacher, worked with the decoration committee. They hung up signs and banners.

Andy carried the toolbox and shopping bag of gerbil food and wood chips to the table. He helped Ms. Roman arrange the prizes on the table. Along with the ones the class had brought in, Ms. Roman and Mr. Williams had brought school pencils, notebooks, and book covers.

Andy put some wood chips and food in each of the jars.

"I know how to handle gerbils," Ms. Roman said. "I'll help you put them in the jars."

Andy was on the other side of the table when Ms. Roman opened the toolbox and reached in.

"Not so wide!" Andy shouted.

Ms. Roman grabbed a gerbil by the tail and took it out. She gently dropped it into a jar and twisted on the lid.

Andy leaped across the table to close the box. But before he could, five gerbils climbed up, looked at Andy and Ms. Roman, quickly got out, and ran across the gym floor.

"Help! A mouse!" Nicole Adams shouted.

"Help! Help!" the children working on the ring-toss game yelled, and ran out of the gym.

Nicole Adams climbed up onto the parallel bars and sat there.

One boy rolled a sign into a tube and called, "Here, mousy, mousy! You like tunnels. Here, mousy, mousy!"

Another boy grabbed a broom, stood in the middle of the gym, and shouted, "Get over here, you mice!" Then he swung the broom.

"Hey!" Mr. Dexter shouted. "Be careful with that broom or you'll hurt someone."

"Give me that!" Mr. Williams said as he grabbed the broom.

"I'm sorry," Ms. Roman told Andy. "What should we do now?"

Andy said, "There's some food left. I'll put it in the prize box. Maybe they'll come for it."

Andy poured the food into the box and then put

it on the floor turned sideways, so the gerbils could get in.

Tamika and Bruce hurried to Andy and asked, "What can we do to help?"

"You can put the gerbils that haven't escaped into the jars. Very carefully open the toolbox, reach in, and grab a tail. Then close the box before any get out."

Bruce looked at Tamika.

"We can do that," Tamika said.

Andy went to the center of the gym and stood next to Mr. Dexter. "These are gerbils," Andy called out. "They're pets. They won't hurt you."

"Just tell us where they are," Mr. Dexter added loudly, "and we'll catch them."

Andy looked around the gym. A few of his classmates were sitting on tables. Some were by the door to the gym and looking in. One girl had a beanbag and was ready to throw it, to scare away the gerbils.

A gerbil ran past the girl with the beanbag, toward the parallel bars.

Bam!

She threw a beanbag at it.

She missed the gerbil and hit Nicole Adams.

"Hey," Nicole yelled, and clutched her heart. "I've been beaned!"

The gerbil ran right into the prize box and began eating the food. Andy reached in, grabbed its tail, and put it into a jar.

"Over here! Over here!" a boy in the corner yelled.

A gerbil was running right toward him.

Mr. Dexter and Andy ran toward the gerbil. The gerbil stopped, turned, and ran the other way, right to Stacy Ann Jackson.

The gerbil looked up at Stacy Ann Jackson. She looked down at the gerbil, smiled, and before the gerbil could run away, she grabbed its tail. She held it in her hands, petted it, and said, "Come with me. I won't hurt you."

Stacy Ann carried the gerbil to the prize table. Bruce unscrewed the lid off a jar, and Stacy Ann dropped the gerbil in.

"Hey!" a boy shouted as he held his backpack upside down and shook it. "Get out of there!"

Books, papers, a few broken pencils, two half-eaten sandwiches, an apple core, and a gerbil fell out of the backpack. The gerbil scrambled to its feet and went straight to the apple core.

Andy grabbed the gerbil by its tail with one hand and the apple core with the other. The gerbil was still eating when Andy dropped the gerbil and the apple core into a jar and Bruce screwed the lid on.

"We're almost done with the other gerbils," Bruce told Andy. "Tamika opens the box, takes one out, and puts it in the jar. I open and close the jars. We're a team."

"There's one! There's one!" Ms. Roman shouted, and pointed.

Ms. Roman was near the beanbag-toss table. She ran after the gerbil. Mr. Dexter and Mr. Williams were near the parallel bars. They ran toward the gerbil. Andy ran, too, from the prize table.

The children in the gym stopped whatever they were doing and watched. The gerbil stopped, too, and looked around, bewildered, as four people from different directions ran toward it.

Ms. Roman reached down for the gerbil, tripped, and landed on her stomach.

Andy's classmates laughed.

Mr. Dexter and Mr. Williams tripped on Ms. Roman's outstretched arms and fell, too. Andy dove to get out of their way and slid across the

floor right into the gerbil. He grabbed it by the tail and held it up in triumph.

His classmates applauded.

Andy slowly got up and carried the gerbil to the prize table. Bruce held out an open jar, and Andy dropped the gerbil in. Then Bruce screwed on the lid.

Mr. Dexter and Mr. Williams got up slowly. Then they helped Ms. Roman up.

Ms. Roman looked around the room.

"Well, that's it," she declared. "We got them all. Now, let's set up the carnival."

"Andy," Bruce whispered, "we have one empty jar. There's still one gerbil on the loose."

Andy looked around the room. Nicole Adams had come off the parallel bars. Children were no longer hiding in the corner, and the ones who had left the gym were coming back in.

"I'll hide the jar," Andy whispered. "We'll keep it a secret that one is missing."

Andy put the empty jar in the toolbox.

"I'll put some food out," Andy whispered to Bruce and Tamika, "so the missing gerbil will have plenty to eat."

Tamika and Bruce returned to the beanbag-toss table. The other children returned to theirs.

Andy filled his pockets with gerbil food. He walked around the gym and looked at all the games being set up. And whenever he thought no one was watching him, he sprinkled some gerbil food under the game tables. When his pockets were empty, he returned to the prize table. Ms. Roman was there, waiting for him.

"I'm sorry," Ms. Roman told Andy. "I should have been more careful."

Andy remembered how good he had felt when he'd slid across the floor, grabbed the gerbil, and his classmates applauded.

"That's OK," Andy told Ms. Roman. "It was fun chasing after them."

She asked Andy to take care of the gerbils and the other prizes.

When the carnival was ready, Ms. Roman and Mr. Dexter opened the doors to the gym, and lots of children came in to play the games. Many of the younger ones had come with their parents. Andy waited for them to come for prizes. It took five WINNER tickets to win a gerbil.

A woman who was holding a small boy's hand came to Andy's table. Andy smiled at the boy. The boy stuck his tongue out at Andy.

What a brat, Andy thought.

The woman put seven WINNER tickets on the table and asked, "What can we get?"

Andy showed her volume L of the encyclopedia, the old football, the comic books, and the school supplies.

"What about those animals?" the boy asked.

Andy told him, "You don't want one."

"Yes I do!" the boy shouted.

"My son wants an animal," the woman said.

Andy took a Gerbil Contract from his backpack and gave it to the boy. "First, you have to sign this," Andy told him.

The boy read it slowly and said, "I'm not signing any contract!"

"I'm sorry," Andy told him, "you must sign it before you get a gerbil."

"I want an animal!" the boy shouted.

The woman read the contract and asked, "Who's in charge here?"

"My teacher is," Andy said, and pointed to Ms. Roman.

The woman hurried to Ms. Roman. She left the boy with Andy. The boy looked at Andy, stuck out his tongue, then grabbed a jar and shook it.

"Hey," Andy said, and took the jar away from him. "Why did you do that? How would you like it if you were in a jar and someone shook you?"

Andy unscrewed the lid and took the gerbil out. He held it and petted it. When he was sure it wasn't hurt, he returned it to the jar.

Ms. Roman and the woman came to the prize table.

"He shook one of the jars," Andy said, and pointed to the boy. "And he wouldn't sign this."

Andy showed Ms. Roman the contract.

She read it.

"This is a good idea," she told Andy. Then she told the woman, "Andrew is right. We're only giving gerbils to people who will provide them with a good home. Since your son won't sign an agreement, it's clear he shouldn't be given a gerbil."

Ms. Roman counted the WINNER tickets and gave the woman seven pencils.

The woman showed her son the pencils and asked, "Are these OK?"

The boy first looked at Andy. Then he looked at Ms. Roman.

"Yeah," he said, and took the pencils from his mother. "I guess so."

"I'll stay with you," Ms. Roman told Andy after the woman and her son had gone. "And before anyone gets a gerbil, I'll make him or her sign one of your agreements."

Later, while Ms. Roman was giving out a prize, Andy saw something moving between her shoes—the missing gerbil!

Andy didn't know what to do. He couldn't crawl between her legs and get it. He waited.

When Ms. Roman turned, he dropped some gerbil food on the floor. Then, when the gerbil stopped to eat, Andy reached down and grabbed it by its tail.

Ms. Roman turned and saw Andy and the gerbil.

"Please, put it back in a jar," she told him. "If it gets loose and I chase after it, I might fall and make a big fool of myself again."

"You didn't make such a big fool of yourself," Andy said as he took the jar from the toolbox and put the gerbil in.

By the end of the carnival there were only three

gerbils left and volume L of the encyclopedia. Andy let Bruce choose the gerbil he wanted. Andy gave the other two to Ms. Roman. He knew she would be good to them. *And maybe,* he thought, *she can teach the gerbils how to divide fractions. She certainly couldn't teach me how to do it.*

Ms. Roman held up her two jars and told the gerbils inside them, "I'm taking you home with me. I'll buy you a nice big tank and lots of toys. Now, won't that be nice?"

The gerbils didn't answer.

Poor Ms. Roman, Andy thought. *First, she has a room full of students who can't answer her questions, and now she has two jars of gerbils who can't.*

Mr. Russell came and drove Andy and Tamika home.

"Tonight the Perlmans are taking me to a restaurant," Tamika said in the car. "It will be our good-bye dinner."

"That's really nice," Mr. Russell said.

He stopped in front of the Perlmans' house. "And tomorrow," he told Tamika before she got out of the car, "after we get back from the airport, you'll eat dinner with us. It will be our hello dinner."

Chapter 10
Welcome Tamika!

In school the next day, Ms. Roman told the class how pleased the people at the soup kitchen were to receive their donation. "It was a good carnival," she told the class, "and we did a good deed, helping to support a kitchen that feeds people who are hungry."

At lunchtime Andy quickly ate his sandwich.

"Hurry," he told Tamika and Bruce. "I have two cans of cat food, Chicken Delight and Salmon Surprise. I'm going to open both and see which one Cobalt goes to first."

As soon as Tamika and Bruce finished their lunches, they went outside.

Andy, Tamika, and Bruce looked behind the trash cans, but Cobalt wasn't there. They looked for her by the swings and the basketball courts. As they searched the playground and didn't find her, Andy began to worry that something might have happened to Cobalt. Then, at last, he saw her in the corner behind the sandbox. She was playing with Stacy Ann Jackson.

Stacy Ann was dangling a piece of purple wool, and Cobalt was waving her paw at it.

"Hey! What are you doing with Cobalt?" Andy asked.

"This isn't Cobalt," Stacy Ann said. "This is Ubastet, and she's lonely. She likes it when I play with her."

"Uba what?" Andy asked.

"Ubastet. I named her after the Egyptian cat goddess. People in ancient Egypt loved cats. They even prayed to them."

"They did?" Andy asked.

"Yes," Stacy Ann said, and petted the kitten. "And I love cats, too. I was real happy when I found Ubastet. Now I have someone to play with and talk to during lunch."

Andy, Tamika, and Bruce watched as Stacy Ann petted the kitten some more.

Tamika looked at Andy and Bruce. Then she looked at Stacy Ann and said, "You can talk to us."

"I can?" Stacy Ann asked.

"She can sit with us, too. Can't she?" Bruce asked Andy.

Tamika and Stacy Ann Jackson looked at Andy.

"Hey, why is everyone looking at me?" Andy asked. But he knew why they were looking. They wanted him to agree that Stacy Ann Jackson could sit with him, Tamika, and Bruce at lunch.

Andy remembered how some girls had screamed and run from the gerbils when they got loose in the gym. But Stacy Ann caught one and had even been gentle with it. And she was playing so nicely with Cobalt, or Ubastet.

Andy remembered his favorite saying. *"People who are nice to animals are nice people."* And Stacy Ann Jackson *was* nice to animals.

"You can sit with us," Andy told her, "if you don't tell us how smart you are, or what grades you got, or that I should pay attention in class."

Stacy Ann Jackson smiled.

"I won't," she said. "And I don't think you're stupid. I think you're clever and know lots of things I don't know, like what global warming is."

"OK! OK! Enough of what you think," Andy said.

Then Andy opened both cans of cat food. The kitten ate the Salmon Surprise first. Then she ate the Chicken Delight.

While the cat ate, Stacy Ann told Andy, "We can call her Cobalt. It's a nice name."

"Or we can call her Ubastet," Andy said.

"How about Fluffy?" Bruce asked.

"Oh no!" Andy and Stacy Ann said together.

"How about Ubolt," Tamika suggested. "It's a combination of Ubastet and Cobalt."

"No," Stacy Ann said. "Ubolt is a really strange name. It sounds like something a plumber might use to fix a toilet. We'll call her Cobalt. I like that name."

Stacy Ann told Andy that she lived near the school. She said Andy could feed Cobalt on school days, and she promised to feed her on weekends and during school vacations.

When the bell rang, Andy, Tamika, Bruce, and Stacy Ann returned to class together.

During the geography lesson, Andy watched Stacy Ann listen intently to Ms. Roman.

How can she listen to all this stuff about oceans and mountains, Andy wondered. *It's all so boring.* Then he remembered that Stacy Ann Jackson liked animals. *She's not all bad.*

On the bus ride home, Tamika didn't talk much. She just stared out the window.

"Dad said he would be home early," Andy told her when they got off the bus. "Just knock on our door when you're ready to go to the airport."

When Andy got in the house, he said to Rachel, "Let's hang up the signs now."

"No," Rachel told him. "I'm doing my homework now."

"Then I'll decorate the house," Andy said.

"No," Rachel told him again. "We want to surprise Tamika. If we do it now, she'll see the signs and cake when she comes to tell you the Perlmans are ready."

"When she knocks on the door," Andy said, "I'll go outside. She won't see anything."

"Listen," Rachel said impatiently, "you and Dad get to go to the airport, and Mom and I are decorating the house. That's fair and that's it!"

Andy went to his room. He threw his schoolbooks on his bed and sat there, next to the window, and did his homework.

Every time Andy heard a car drive by or someone walk by, he looked out. He was anxious to go to the airport and even more anxious for Tamika to move into his house.

He was studying history when he saw Tamika walk over carrying a large suitcase. Andy raced out of his room and down the steps to the front door. He opened it just as Tamika was about to ring the bell.

"It's early," Andy said. "My dad's not home yet."

Tamika said, "We're not ready to go to the airport. I'm just bringing over my things."

"Hi," Rachel called from the kitchen. Then she joined Andy and Tamika at the front door.

Tamika lifted the suitcase with both hands and carried it into the house.

Andy asked, "Is it heavy?"

Tamika nodded.

Andy said, "I'll carry it."

He struggled to pick up the suitcase.

"Maybe we should both carry it," he told Tamika.

Andy and Tamika both grabbed the handle and followed Rachel to her room.

"Your bed is the one by the window," Rachel said when they entered her room. "I made room in my closet for your things, and I emptied part of my dresser."

"Thanks," Tamika said.

Andy went to the Perlmans' and helped carry the rest of Tamika's things. Then he and Tamika sat on the Perlmans' front porch and waited for Mr. Russell to come home and for the Perlmans to be ready to go to the airport.

They sat quietly for a while. Then Tamika told Andy, "Miriam said she'll bring me lots of coins and stamps from South America, and she'll send me picture postcards and souvenirs."

Andy said, "And maybe Dr. Perlman will send you a South American barber's chair."

"Yeah," Tamika said. "Maybe."

They were quiet again, until Andy's parents came home. Mrs. Russell got out of the car and went into the house. Then Mr. Russell drove his car into the Perlmans' driveway.

HONK! HONK!

Andy ran to the car. Tamika went inside to tell the Perlmans that Mr. Russell was there.

Mr. Russell helped the Perlmans load three large suitcases and two boxes into the trunk and onto the roof of his car.

"Don't you just love going to the airport?" Mrs. Perlman asked Tamika as they got into the car. "You get to see people coming from all over the world."

Tamika didn't answer, and Andy knew that even if she loved going to the airport, she didn't love saying good-bye to the Perlmans.

"I like to look at people just getting off a plane, at their clothes and their luggage," Mrs. Perlman said, "and guess where they came from."

Andy sat in the back of the car with Tamika and Mrs. Perlman. During the drive, Mrs. Perlman talked and tried to cheer up Tamika.

"I'll bet we forgot to pack something really important," Mrs. Perlman said, "like my reading glasses. You know, without them I have to hold things really far away to read them."

She looked at Tamika and asked, "Could you imagine trying to read a magazine that way on a crowded airplane? Now that would be funny!"

Tamika didn't respond.

"Do you remember when you read the menu to me at the restaurant?" Mrs. Perlman asked. "I felt like a little child."

As Tamika turned to look out the window, Andy saw how upset she was and was sorry the Perlmans had to go away.

Tamika stayed with the Perlmans while they checked their luggage and showed their tickets to the ticket agent. She walked with them upstairs to the waiting area. Andy and his dad followed behind them.

"Sit with me," Mr. Russell told Andy.

Andy and Mr. Russell sat across from Tamika and the Perlmans. Andy watched Mrs. Perlman reach out and take Tamika's hand and hold it between hers.

Dr. Perlman started to say something, but his wife stopped him. "No. Quiet," she said softly, and they sat there, quietly waiting.

When their flight was announced, Dr. and Mrs. Perlman hugged Tamika for a long time.

"Good-bye," Dr. Perlman said, and went through the metal detector and walked toward the gate.

Mrs. Perlman petted Tamika's cheek, whispered, "You take care," and then followed Dr. Perlman through the metal detector.

Tamika stood there for a while.

Let's go already, Andy thought. *I want to get home and eat cake and cookies.* But he didn't say it. He just waited until Tamika was ready.

When they were in the car, leaving the airport, a large airplane about to land flew right above them.

Without thinking, Mr. Russell bent his head down a little. Then he laughed at himself and said, "That seemed pretty close."

"Yeah," Andy said. "I felt I could almost reach up and touch it."

Tamika didn't react to the airplane. She just sat by herself in the backseat of the car and stared out the window.

"Well, here we are," Mr. Russell said awhile later when he stopped the car in front of the house.

Andy got out, ran to the front door, and rang the bell.

"I have a key," his father told him as he unlocked the door.

"I know," Andy said. "It's just that I promised Rachel I would warn her when we came home."

Rachel and Mrs. Russell were coming to the front door when Andy and Mr. Russell walked in.

"Where's Tamika?" Rachel asked.

"She's just getting out of the car," Andy said.

Andy looked at the balloon pictures, the signs, and the banner—THE RUSSELL FAMILY LOVES TAMIKA ANDERSON!—and smiled. The house really looked great.

Andy, Rachel, and their parents stood by the door and waited.

Tamika slowly walked through the doorway, stepped in, and stopped. She read all the signs and the banner. Then she looked at the Russells.

"This is so nice," she said.

She wiped her eyes and then hugged Andy, Rachel, and their parents.

"Oh my," she said after she hugged Mrs. Russell. She looked at Mrs. Russell's stomach and said, "I hope I didn't hurt the baby."

"I'm fine," Mrs. Russell told her, "and the baby is fine."

"We're *all* fine," Andy declared, "and hungry. Let's eat some cake."

They all followed Andy into the kitchen. He held up the cake and showed everyone that WELCOME TAMIKA! was written on it. Then Mrs. Russell cut the cake and gave everyone a piece.

Rachel asked her parents, "Do you think the baby likes cake?"

"Sure he . . . ," Mr. Russell said, and then quickly stopped.

"Sure *she* does," Mrs. Russell said.

"It's a boy!" Andy shouted. "When Dad wasn't thinking, he said 'he.'"

"No, it's a girl," Rachel told him. "Mom said 'she.'"

"Oh, what's the difference?" Tamika asked. "I would just love it if my mother had a baby, and I wouldn't care if it was a boy or a girl."

"She's right," Mrs. Russell said.

Andy knew Tamika didn't like being an only child. He decided having Rachel as his sister was better than nothing. And having another sister would be fine, too.

The Russells and Tamika ate the cake and cookies. Andy and Rachel drank soda. Mr. and Mrs. Russell had tea. And Mrs. Russell took a container of skim milk from the refrigerator and poured a cup of it for Tamika.

"I spoke to Mrs. Perlman," Mrs. Russell told Tamika, "and she said this is what you drink. She also said you like carrot juice. We have some of that, too."

The Russells and Tamika talked for a while. Then Tamika taught them some of the Perlmans' favorite songs.

Tamika thanked the Russells as she helped them clean up after their party. "I really feel at home."

Later that evening, at dinner, Mrs. Russell said, "Your father and I have something to tell you."

Andy looked at his father.

"Yes," Mr. Russell said. "We just can't keep this secret any longer. It's too hard for me to remember to call our baby 'it.' "

Mr. Russell looked at Mrs. Russell.

They both smiled.

"We decided," Mrs. Russell said, "to tell you the baby's gender."

Andy's parents looked at each other and smiled again.

"So, tell us already," Andy said.

"The baby is a boy," Mr. Russell announced.

"YES!" Andy shouted.

"And we're naming him Evan," Mrs. Russell said.

Andy clapped his hands and said, "That's fair. Now Rachel will have two brothers, me and Evan, and I'll have two sisters, Rachel and Tamika."

Everyone was quiet for a moment. Then Tamika said softly, "I won't stay here forever. My parents will be better soon, and I'll live with them again."

"I know," Andy told her, "but you'll still be my sister. You'll always be my sister."

"Thank you," Tamika said.

There were tears in her eyes.

Andy looked down at the noodles and cheese on his plate.

"Hey!" he said. "I can't eat noodles and cheese now. I just found out I'm getting a brother. We have to celebrate."

"Well," Mrs. Russell said. "We have some cake left."

"And some cookies," Mr. Russell added.

While they ate cake and cookies, Tamika said, "You know what? I think when the baby comes home from the hospital, we should bake a cake and cookies again, and make banners and signs and hang them up."

She looked first at Andy and then at Rachel and said, "We should make Evan feel welcome in his new home." She smiled. "Making someone feel welcome is nice. It's so very nice."

Turn the page for a sneak peek
at Andy's next adventure....

Two new siblings, one new friend, and a few less gerbils! Things are looking up for Andy now, right?

Well, not quite.

School is even more tiresome than usual. With Ms. Roman out sick, Andy's class is in an uproar. And even worse, when someone starts playing tricks on the mean substitute teacher, guess whom she accuses?

Read *School Trouble for Andy Russell* to find out why Andy won't be the only one getting into trouble now!